Chapter 1

It was a busy and bustling Saturday morning in Turtleville. Chloe Coral and her starfish pal, Pam, had been up since the crack of dawn preparing delicious MER-MUFFINS for the family cafe, Turtleville Tearooms.

During school holidays Chloe and Pam helped Grandmer Coral with the running of the Tearooms. Chloe was an absolute WHIZ in the kitchen!

'Chloeeeeeeeee! Some VIPs on table fifteen need more SEA FOAMUCCINOS,' yelled Grandmer Coral. 'Be a DEAR LITTLE DORY and float some over.'

'NOW?!' spluttered Pam. 'Can't you see we've got our FINS FULL here, Carol?'

'Relax, Pam,' chuckled Chloe. 'Coming right up, Grandmer. Who are the VERY IMPORTANT PRAWNS?'

'Oh, I don't know, but they need their drinks so CHOP CHOP,' Carol said with a wink.

'Very Important Prawns,' grumbled Pam. 'What NONSENSE! They should wait their turn like all the other customers.'

As they hurried through the kitchen door, and before Pam could GRUMBLE and GRIPE anymore, Chloe gasped. 'PIPPING PIPIS!'

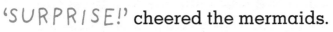

'SURPRISE!' cheered the mermaids.

Chloe attended the local school in Turtleville, but her friends – Willow, Sophia and Olivia – went to different schools across the reef. It had been weeks since they had seen each other. Chloe was THRILLED to have the gang back together.

'What are you all doing here?!' giggled Chloe as she hugged her mermates. 'I didn't think you'd be back in Turtleville till this afternoon.'

'We couldn't resist surprising you,' gushed Sophia.

'And Bruce was desperate for Grandmer Coral's SEAWEED SCROLLS,' giggled Olivia.

'Would you mind leaving some scrolls for the rest of us, please?' snapped Smedley, disapprovingly.

'Don't start, you two,' tutted Willow. 'Now we're all together we can make some MERMAZING plans for the holidays!'

Chloe and Pam settled down at the table with their mermates, ready to discuss their upcoming adventures.

'As long as this holiday doesn't involve MAGIC PEARLS or TALENT SHOWS, I'll be happy,' grumbled Smedley.

'Oh, Smeds! You're such a STICK IN THE MUDSKIPPER,' chuckled Sophia. 'The talent show was great fun.'

'Oooh, I know what we can do,' said Olivia. 'Let's have a TAIL TENNIS TOURNAMENT.'

'I'm in,' squealed Willow. 'What about you, Chloe?'

'Sounds MERMAZING!'

'Now, now, what sounds MERMAZING?'
Grandmer Coral floated over to the mermaids.
'I am so happy to see you girls back in town.
I still remember when you were tiny merbies.
It brings a tear to my eye.'

'Grandmer, you're such a SOPPY SQUID,'
said Chloe, blushing.

'Thank you for all the delicious food, Mrs Coral,'
said Smedley.

Grandmer Coral chuckled. 'You're quite welcome.
Oh and that reminds me, Chloe and I have been
working on a delicious new cake for our holiday
menu and I want you to be the first to try it.'

PING!

'Oooh, that's the oven,' said Grandmer Coral,
excitedly. 'It must be ready!'

As Grandmer Coral floated off into the kitchen, a humungous *BOOM* filled the tearooms.

'OH. MY. *POSEIDON!*' cried Olivia. 'What on earth was that?!'

Grandmer Coral emerged from the kitchen in a cloud of smoke.

'Erm, Chloe dear,' coughed Grandmer Coral.
'I'm not quite sure what happened, but I think
the oven may have BLOWN UP!'

Chapter 2

Grandmer Coral had proudly run the Turtleville Tearooms for as long as Chloe could remember. It was Chloe's home and she loved it with all her heart. Every morning the Tearooms would be filled with CHATTER and CHEER as townsfolk enjoyed yummy SEA FOAMUCCINOS.

But the morning after the EXPLOSION, there was no CHATTER and no CHEER. Turtleville Tearooms were CLOSED for business.

The explosion had DESTROYED the kitchen. Grandmer Coral knew she couldn't fix this mess on her own so she called Doug, Turtleville's trusty builder, to inspect the damage.

'What do you think, Doug?' asked Grandmer Coral.

Doug paused and scratched his chin. 'What would you like to hear first? The GOOD news or the BAD news?'

'GOOD news, please!' replied Pam.

'Good news is, I can fix it.'

'And the B-B-BAD news?' stammered Chloe.

'Well, that WOBBLY wall over there needs sorting otherwise the whole place will come CRASHING down. And that's just the start.' Doug sighed. 'You'll need the entire kitchen replaced, not to mention a new oven.'

'That sounds . . .' Grandmer Coral gulped nervously, '. . . EXPENSIVE.'

Doug totted up the numbers. 'All in all, this will cost TWO THOUSAND SAND DOLLARS.'

'PIPPING PIPIS!'
gasped Grandmer Coral.

'Sorry, Mrs Coral,' said Doug. 'I don't like to be a BIG DEPRESSING DUGONG, but your only options are to make the repairs or close the doors to the Tearooms . . . FOR GOOD.'

As Doug left, Grandmer Coral slumped onto one of the upside-down pots on the kitchen floor.

Chloe was worried. Surely they wouldn't have to close the Tearooms. Would they?

'It's okay, Grandmer,' said Chloe. 'We can get Doug to fix everything and we'll be back in business in no time.'

'Oh, my PRETTY LITTLE PUFFERFISH,' said Grandmer Coral as she hugged Chloe. 'I'm afraid it's not that easy. I used the emergency savings to go on that baking course in Stingray Sands. I don't have enough money.'

'What are you saying, Grandmer?'

Carol pulled a hanky from her sleeve and dabbed her eyes. 'It's the last thing I want to do,' she said between snivels, 'but I think we will have to CLOSE TURTLEVILLE TEAROOMS.'

'CLOSE THE TEAROOMS!' gasped Chloe and Pam.

'I'm so sorry, my DARLING DORY,' Carol sobbed as she blew her nose loudly. 'We've got no choice.'

With more SNIFFLES and SOBS, Grandmer
Coral swam upstairs for a lie down, leaving
Chloe and Pam in the WRECKED and
RUINED kitchen.

'Okay, Pam,' said Chloe. 'Grandmer needs our
help. We have to find a way to fix this!'

'But what can we do?' Pam sighed, defeated. 'You heard Doug, TWO THOUSAND SAND DOLLARS! We don't have that kind of money floating about the place.'

'We don't,' said Chloe. 'But all we need is a MERMAZING PLAN, and I know exactly who can help us.'

Chapter 3

If there was one thing Chloe and her mermates were good at, it was coming up with MERMAZING PLANS. Chloe knew she could rely on them to help think of a way to save Turtleville Tearooms from closing down.

All it took was an urgent mermail asking them to meet at Turtleville Lagoon and the mermaids were there in a JELLYFISH JIFFY.

'YOU CAN'T CLOSE TURTLEVILLE TEAROOMS!' cried the mermaids.

This was exactly the reaction Chloe had
expected. Turtleville Tearooms wasn't just her
home, it was special to all of them. Ever since
they were tiny merbies, they had spent the
holidays there and made lots of happy memories.

A Turtleville without the Tearooms wasn't
Turtleville at all.

'I know,' said Chloe. 'But my grandmer can't afford to make the repairs.'

'Which is why we sent you all the urgent mermail,' added Pam as she revealed a big board to brainstorm ideas. 'We need a MERMAZING PLAN and we need it NOW if we want to save the Tearooms.'

Sophia sighed. 'I wish we had some of Grandmer Coral's delicious MER-MUFFINS to help us think.'

'Oooh and a SEA JELLY SLICE!' said Willow.

'Talking about tasty treats from Turtleville Tearooms is not getting us any closer to working out how to save it,' snapped Smedley. 'It's just making me hungry!'

'Okay, so Grandmer needs money to pay Doug,'
Chloe said as she wrote on the board. 'So
we have to think of a way to RAISE TWO
THOUSAND SAND DOLLARS.'

Everyone nodded in agreement, but still no one
had a plan.

The lagoon was silent as the mermaids UMMMED and AHHHED. They'd never had to think up a plan like THIS before.

'Anyone?' prompted Chloe.

Suddenly, Bruce broke the silence. 'That Doug is a SNEAKY SEA SLUG,' he grumbled. 'He should do the work for free!'

Pam gave Bruce a disapproving nudge. 'It's not Doug's fault the oven exploded.'

'All I'm saying is, the amount of SEA FOAMUCCINOS he's GUZZLED and SEAWEED SCROLLS he's SCOFFED over the years, he probably owes Mrs Coral money!' huffed Bruce.

'It doesn't quite work like that, old boy,' said Smedley. 'Instead of playing the BLAME GAME, we've got to put our TAILS TOGETHER and work out HOW we can raise the money.'

'What about a BAKE SALE?' suggested Frida. 'Seeing as we're raising money for the Tearooms, it makes sense that YUMMY cakes should be involved.'

'I like your thinking, Frida,' chirped Chloe.

'OH. MY. POSEIDON! I've got it!' shrieked Sophia. 'A FUNDRAISER BAKE-OFF COMPETITION!'

The mermaids stared at her like a bunch of MUDDLE-HEADED HERRINGS.

'A fundraiser *what*-off?' replied Pam.

'Miss Sophia, you CLEVER CLAM!' cheered
Smedley.

'Thanks, Smeds.' Sophia winked at her seahorse
pal. 'So, I'm thinking out loud right now, but we
could make it a TOWN EVENT!'

'Whoa, whoa, whoa! Hold your SEAHORSES,'
said Chloe. 'Just HOW exactly will we raise
money?'

'SIMPLE!' said Sophia. 'We can get some of the sizzling cooks in town to show off their BAKING SKILLS, then we will sell tickets to everyone who wants to come along to watch and eat all the delicious cakes. The crowd can even help judge the competition! Each ticket will be a donation of TEN SAND DOLLARS for the SAVE THE TURTLEVILLE TEAROOMS FUND.'

MERMAZING PLAN
1. ~~FIND MONEY~~
2. ~~MAKE DOUG WORK FOR FREE~~
3. BAKE-OFF!

'I LOVE IT!' cheered Willow.

'MERMAZING!' added Olivia.

'I can't wait to tell Grandmer Coral!' sang Chloe.

'But just one thing . . .' Chloe said with a sigh,
'how will we get the whole town to come along?'

'Why don't we announce it at the TOWN
MEETING tomorrow night?' said Pam.
'I bet everyone will be so excited!'

'I hope so,' said Chloe, sadly.

'Of course they will,' said Willow. 'No one wants
Turtleville Tearooms to close.'

'Right then, now we've got our MERMAZING PLAN,' said Olivia, 'we better work out what we're going to say at the town meeting!'

Chapter 4

The Turtleville Town Meeting was held every Monday evening, and without fail the whole town was there at six o'clock on the dot. The mermaids couldn't wait to tell everyone about the BAKE-OFF. But Chloe was also VERY nervous because Turtleville's mayor, Herb, was a HUFFY OLD HERMIT CRAB. If he didn't like her plan, there would be NO bake-off.

Unfortunately, the meeting was already off to a BAD start. Kirk, the town's cranky krill, was having his weekly grumble about law and order in Turtleville. Every week Kirk told Constable Crabigail Crick that she should hire him as her deputy.

'KIRK! We go over this every meeting. Constable Crabigail does not need a deputy constable. Please stop bothering her for the job,' Herb said finally as he looked at the meeting list. 'Moving on. Are there any other town matters to discuss?'

Sophia nudged a nervous Chloe before shouting out, 'YES! We have a very important matter to raise.'

Herb looked down at the crowd. 'Is that little Sophia Seashell?'

'Yes, Herb. But it's Chloe Coral who would like to talk.' Sophia nudged Chloe again.

'Well, Miss Coral, we haven't got all night,' barked Herb. 'WHAT IS IT?'

Chloe slowly made her way to the front of the hall.

'Well, as you k-k-know. The T-Tearooms had a l-l-little e-explosion and, well . . .'

'Spit it out!' heckled Kirk. 'You're not a STUTTERING STICKLEBACK!'

Pam glared at the cranky krill and swam on stage to help Chloe.

'After the AWFUL OVEN EXPLOSION, our beloved Turtleville Tearooms has been DESTROYED,' Pam said as she perched on Chloe's shoulder. 'The place is a MESS and if we don't raise the TWO THOUSAND SAND DOLLARS to fix it, Carol Coral will have to close the Tearooms ... FOR GOOD!'

Gasps of dismay filled the hall and Grandmer Coral could be heard SNIFFING and SOBBING from the front row.

'B-b-but we have a MERMAZING PLAN,' said Chloe, feeling a little braver, 'and with your help we can save the Tearooms.'

'Okay, Miss Coral. You've got my attention,' grumbled Herb. 'I can speak for the whole town when I say none of us want to see the Turtleville Tearooms close.'

'Agreed! I've been SO CRANKY the last few days without my morning SEA FOAMUCCINO,' said Kirk. 'Let's hear this MERMAZING PLAN then.'

'We need to raise money for the repairs so my grandmer can get back to doing what she loves.' Chloe took a deep breath and continued, 'So, my mermates and I thought we could put on a FUNDRAISER BAKE-OFF!'

Excited murmurs filled the room.

'How's this fundraiser bake-off going to work then?' Kirk called out.

'One thing at a time, Kirk,' snapped Herb. 'Let Miss Coral explain.'

Chloe and Pam excitedly told the town all about the bake-off. With the mention of delicious cake everyone seemed keen to hear more. Even HUFFY OLD HERB was listening intently.

'It's going to be a full day of FISHTASTIC FUNDRAISING FUN!' sang Chloe.

'If everyone buys a ticket, we can get the Tearooms up and running again!' added Pam.

The hall ERUPTED into happy CHEERS. This had gone far better than Chloe had expected.

'The bake-off will be held in the Town Square on Saturday,' said Herb. 'All in favour, say "AYE".'

But before anyone could say a word, a sickly sweet voice from the back of the hall called out, 'I have something to say, if you don't mind?'

Everyone turned around and an elegant mermaid SWISHED her way to the stage.

'BARBARA BARNACLE!' Grandmer Coral groaned. 'What in FLAPPING FLOUNDERS are YOU doing here?'

Barbara Barnacle used to be Grandmer Coral's BESTEST MERMATE in the whole wide waters. Until one day Barbara stole all of Carol's secret family recipes and opened her own cafe, BAB'S BISTRO, in the town across the reef. For years the RUMOUR ON THE RIPTIDE was that Barbara wanted to take over the Tearooms and turn it into another Bab's Bistro!

Chloe knew this was the reason Barbara was back in Turtleville. She was trying to get her hands on the Tearooms.

'What are you doing here, Barbara?' asked
Chloe, suspiciously.

Barbara chuckled as she shooed Chloe and Pam
to the side of the stage. 'Townsfolk of Turtleville,
as a fellow business owner, I am here to offer
support to my friend Carol Coral.'

'You are NOT Carol's friend,'
snorted Pam.

Barbara ignored Pam and Chloe and continued, 'I heard about the TERRIBLE EXPLOSION at the Tearooms and the, AHEM, money troubles you've been having. So I said to myself, "Barbara, you should help this old dear out and take the shop off her hands".'

'My grandmer doesn't need YOUR help,' snapped Chloe. 'We already have a MERMAZING PLAN to save the Tearooms.'

'Yeah, Barbara!' yelled Sophia. 'We've planned a *FISHTASTIC BAKE-OFF* to raise lots of sand dollars for Mrs Coral.'

'BAHAHAHAHAHAHAHAHA!' Barbara cackled loudly. When she finally caught her breath, she said, 'Oh, you SWEET LITTLE SCALLOP. Your bake-off is a DARLING idea, but you'll NEVER raise enough sand dollars.'

'You don't know that!' blurted Smedley.

'Oh, but I do,' replied Barbara as she turned to Grandmer Coral with a smug smile. 'Carol, I'm here to SAVE YOUR TAIL SCALES, can't you see that? Selling the Tearooms to me so I can turn it into another BAB'S BISTRO is your ONLY option.'

'PIPPING PIPIS!' puffed Pam. 'That BARNACLE has got SOME CHEEK!'

'Turtleville doesn't want a BAB'S BISTRO!' cried Olivia.

'You SNEAKY SEA SNAKE!' snapped
Grandmer Coral.

'Settle down!' shouted a flustered Herb.
'Ms Barnacle, as you can see, the townsfolk of
Turtleville want to save the Tearooms. We will
go ahead with Chloe Coral's BAKE-OFF.
I now call this meeting OVER.'

After the meeting the mermaids and Grandmer Coral made their way home.

'Chloe, you were MERMAZING up there,' said Carol. 'And you stood up to that BEASTLY BARBARA!'

'Who are you calling BEASTLY?!' snapped Barbara, making them jump as she appeared from nowhere.

'Barbara,' said Carol, frostily. 'If you think you'll get your greedy mitts on MY Tearooms, you're dreaming! I'd rather be SUCKED INTO A SINKHOLE before I see it turned into a BAB'S BISTRO!'

'We'll see about that,' Barbara said with a sly smile. 'You will regret this! Don't say I didn't warn you.' With a SWISH of her tail she swam away.

'What in BLABBERING BLOBFISH is that supposed to mean?' muttered Willow.

Chloe shrugged. 'Whatever it is, I don't think it's good.'

Chapter 5

Later that evening, the mermaids made their way to Turtleville Lagoon and got to work. The bake-off was in less than a week and they had A LOT to do. Luckily, Pam was a STARFISH with a plan.

Pam's voice BOOMED across the lagoon, 'Okay, I need ALL EYES ON ME and your FULL ATTENTION!'

'The bake-off is in FIVE DAYS,' Pam continued, 'so we need to get our GILLS INTO GEAR and work like we've never worked before! The future of the Tearooms depends on us!'

'To keep us on track,' added Chloe, 'we will follow this TIMETABLE OF TASKS. We can't be LAZY LOBSTERS if we want to be prepared for Saturday and sell lots of tickets.'

'Are you ready?' cried Chloe.

'SHELL YEAH!' cheered the mermaids.

TIMETABLE OF TASKS

MONDAY : GET A GOOD NIGHT SLEEP
TUESDAY: MAKE POSTERS, BANNERS AND SPREAD THE WORD.
WEDNESDAY : SIGN UP DAY !!
THURSDAY : BUILD THE BAKE-OFF TENT.
FRIDAY : MAKE YUMMY CUPCAKES FOR BAKE SALE.

SATURDAY : THE BAKE-OFF !!

Monday's task was EASY-PEASY! With
'Get a good night's sleep' ticked off the list, the
mermaids woke up bright and early, ready for
Tuesday's task . . .

A FISHTASTIC day of making posters and banners for the bake-off.

Wednesday's task was SUPER FUN! Chloe and Willow set up a booth in town and signed up four great contestants for Saturday's competition. Even Kirk the cranky krill fancied his luck!

Thursday's task was a challenge. The mermaids had to set up the Town Square for the big day and they needed HELP! Luckily, with the promise of a SEAWEED SCROLL, Doug Dugong was more than happy to muck in.

Now all that was left to do was . . .

BAKE, BAKE, BAKE!

The mermaids decided they would make
MER-MUFFINS for townsfolk to buy on the
day to help raise a few extra sand dollars.

By Friday evening they were EXHAUSTED!
It definitely didn't feel like their usual holidays,
but none of the mermates cared because they
were going to save Turtleville Tearooms!

Chloe smiled as she ticked off Friday's task
on the timetable. 'We've done EVERYTHING
on the list!'

'WOOHOO!' cheered Olivia.

'Tomorrow is going to be FISHTASTIC!' hollered Sophia.

'I can't WAIT!' added Willow.

'Can we sleep now?' said Smedley with a big yawn.

TIMETABLE OF TASKS

MONDAY : GET A GOOD NIGHT SLEEP ✓
TUESDAY : MAKE POSTERS, BANNERS AND SPREAD THE WORD. ✓
WEDNESDAY : SIGN UP DAY!! ✓
THURSDAY : BUILD THE BAKE-OFF TENT. ✓
FRIDAY : MAKE YUMMY CUPCAKES FOR BAKE SALE. ✓

SATURDAY : THE BAKE-OFF !!

That night Chloe FLOPPED into bed. She was just about to drift off to sleep when a VERY WORRYING thought POPPED into her head.

BARBARA BARNACLE.

The week had WHIZZED by and Chloe had forgotten all about the mean mermaid. But now she couldn't get the SNEAKY SEA TOAD out of her head. As Pam SNOOZED and SNORED, Chloe suddenly remembered the last thing Barbara had said to her grandmer . . . 'You will regret this! Don't say I didn't warn you.'

What had that BOTHERSOME BARNACLE meant? Was she going to ruin the bake-off?

Chloe had no idea. But she had an ICKY feeling in her tummy that Barbara had BIG plans of her own for the bake-off.

Chapter 6

'Wakey-wakey!' sang Pam. 'We don't have time to be SNOOZY SEA SLUGS.'

Chloe groaned as Pam nudged her out of bed. 'I don't think I slept a PERIWINKLE last night. I had the WORST dream that Barbara Barnacle ruined the bake-off.'

'She wouldn't dare,' said Pam.

Chloe hoped Pam was right. Because today was the BIG DAY!

As Chloe and Pam arrived at the Town Square, her mermates were already hard at work.

'Morning, Miss Chloe, Pamela,' Smedley said with a nod. 'We've set up the ovens in the bake-off tent, Sophia has decorated the ticket booth and Willow has made this MARVELLOUS collection box for all the donations and ticket sales.'

'Willow, thank you. It's MERMAZING!' squealed Chloe.

'Bruce is manning the bake-sale booth,' continued Smedley. 'Against my recommendation, I should point out – the GREEDY GUPPY has already SCOFFED FIVE MER-MUFFINS.'

'Well, he won't have time to eat anymore because everyone is starting to arrive!' cried Chloe.

It seemed like everyone in Turtleville had turned up for the bake-off. The Town Square was CLAM-PACKED and the collection box was almost FULL!

'Oh, Chloe, you are my ANGELFISH!' sang Grandmer Coral. 'This really was a MERMAZING plan. I think we will be able to save our Tearooms after all.'

Chloe was HAPPY AS A HALIBUT, and it was finally time for the BAKE-OFF COMPETITION! But unbeknownst to Chloe and her mermates, floating in the shadows and out of sight, was a very UNWELCOME guest ... BARBARA BARNACLE.

'Welcome, everyone, to TURTLEVILLE'S FUNDRAISER BAKE-OFF!' said Chloe. 'Time to meet our contestants. First up, we have the lovely NORMA! With a passion for pastry and all things SWEET, she is going to treat us to some MORE-ISH MANGROVE MACAROONS.'

'Sounds DELICIOUS!' cheered Sophia.
'In kitchen number two we have Turtleville's
FAVOURITE builder, DOUG! He will be
swapping his hammer for a rolling pin and has
promised to WOW THE CROWD with a
PICKLEWEED PIE.'

'My tummy is RUMBLING and we still have TWO MORE contestants,' giggled Willow. 'In kitchen number three, the fabulous JUDY will be serving up a SENSATIONAL SEA JELLY SPONGE.'

'And finally, in kitchen number four, he's PASSIONATE, he's FEISTY, he's ONE IN A KRILLION ... It's KIRK!' boomed Olivia. 'Kirk has refused to reveal what he is baking, but he has told us it will be a SHOWSTOPPER!'

'BAKERS, you have two hours,' said Smedley. 'On your marks ... GET SET ... BAKE!'

The crowd WHOOPED and CHEERED as the bakers worked their way through their recipes. The time seemed to WHIZ by and before long Smedley called the 30-minute warning.

'Who do you think will win?' asked Willow.

'Judy's got my vote,' said Bruce. 'SEA JELLY is ALWAYS A WINNER in my eyes.'

'What about Kirk?' said Frida. 'I can't wait to ...'

Suddenly, something caught Chloe's eye. She saw a SWISH of a tail and a GLIMPSE of a HEADBAND. Was BARBARA BARNACLE here?

But before Chloe could say anything the timer
BUZZED for the END of the bake-off.

'Okay, BAKERS! Show us your bakes!' hollered Pam.

OOOOHS and AAAHHHHS filled the tent as the four contestants revealed their creations.

'Which baker blew you away?' continued Pam.

'Was it NORMA and her MORE-ISH MACAROONS? DOUG and his PERFECT PIE? JUDY and her SUPER-DUPER SPONGE, or did KIRK steal your heart with his . . .' Chloe paused. 'What actually is this, Kirk?'

With a huff, Kirk held up his bake. 'Mine is a one-of-a-kind SEAWEED SCROLL MEGA-CAKE with SEA FOAMUCCINO FROSTING in honour of Turtleville Tearooms.'

Kirk took a bow and the crowd cheered.

'Now it's time for the TASTE TEST!' announced Chloe. 'Have a NIBBLE and vote for your FAVOURITE BAKE!'

While the mermaids collected the voting tokens from the townsfolk, Chloe kept her eyes PEELED for that BOTHERSOME BARNACLE. But she couldn't find her ANYWHERE!

Maybe she hadn't seen her after all. If Barbara really wanted to ruin the bake-off, she would have done it by now. Wouldn't she?

Even though she was still worried, Chloe had more important things to do. It was time to announce the WINNER of the BAKE-OFF!

The crowd went quiet as Chloe and her mermates floated onto the stage.

'Townsfolk of Turtleville, the votes have been counted,' said Chloe. 'This bake was delicious, original and some might even say it is ONE IN A KRILLION! The winner of the bake-off is ... KIRK!'

The whole town erupted into CHEERS.
'Now we have our winner, does that mean we
can eat all the bakes?!' Bruce shouted over
the noise.

'YES, BRUCE!' replied the mermaids.

The bake-off had been a SUCCESS and everyone was STUFFED TO THE GILLS with cake.

'I don't think I have ever eaten so much,' groaned Willow.

'This has been the BEST DAY!' Bruce said as he ate another MER-MUFFIN.

'It has been fun,' giggled Olivia.

'SO FUN!' agreed Sophia.

Chloe sighed. 'I just hope we raised enough sand dollars to save the Tearooms.'

'Let's find out,' Sophia said as she swam off to get the donation box from the ticket booth.

As the mermaids waited for Sophia, Grandmer Coral and Herb came to join them on the picnic blanket.

'Chloe, my CLEVER LITTLE COCKLE, this whole day has been FISHTASTIC!'

'Best event Turtleville has held in years,' said Herb. 'You mermaids have quite the talent for MERMAZING plans.'

At that moment Sophia came WHIZZING through the water, GASPING and PANTING. 'The donations box ... IT'S GONE!'

Chapter 7

'What do you mean, it's GONE?' cried Pam.

'It must be somewhere,' said Grandmer Coral. 'Maybe someone moved it?'

'But who would move it?' spluttered Sophia.

'Oh no!' Chloe gulped nervously. 'I don't think someone moved it, someone's TAKEN it! And I know exactly who it was.'

'Are you saying someone has STOLEN the donations from the bake-off?' sobbed Grandmer Coral.

'Who would do such a thing?' said Herb.

'Someone who doesn't want us to save the Tearooms,' said Chloe. 'And someone who's had their eye on it for years, that's who!'

'BARBARA BARNACLE!' cried Grandmer Coral.

'The one and only,' Chloe said with a nod. 'I thought I saw her just before we announced the winner, but I assumed my mind was playing TRICKY TUNAS on me.'

'Herb! We've got to tell Constable Crabigail Crick! We can't let that BAD BARNACLE get away with this!' shrieked Grandmer Coral.

Luckily, Constable Crabigail was close by, enjoying a slice of Kirk's winning cake.

In a matter of seconds, the CRIME-STOPPING CRAB had the whole town gathered to help find the missing donation box.

'Listen up! We're going to search every NOOK and CRANNY until we find BARBARA BARNACLE. She can't have gone far, so we need to act FAST,' said Crabigail.

'We have already searched the Town Square,' said Smedley. 'And there is no sign of her at Turtleville Lagoon.'

'What about Cape Kelp Forest?' suggested Willow.

'Good thinking, Miss Wave. Everyone, TO THE FOREST!' hollered Crabigail. 'Spread out and keep your eyes peeled for CLUES.'

'I should have known Barbara would do something to ruin the bake-off,' grumbled Chloe.

'Over here!' Frida yelled. She was holding what looked like a piece of cloth in her tentacle. 'I think I found a CLUE.'

'That's Barbara's HEADBAND,' gasped Chloe.

'SHUSH!' said Smedley. 'Can you hear that?'

The forest was silent. But then . . .

'HELLOOOOO? HEEELLLLP!' called a voice in the distance.

'That voice sounds VERY familiar,' said Bruce.

'Mermates, I think we've found Barbara,' Chloe said, smiling.

With a FLICK and a SWISH of their tails the mermates WHIZZED through the water.

And there she was, stuck in the seaweed slime with her tail TANGLED and TWISTED in SWAMP GRASS.

'HA! We've caught you RED HERRING HANDED!' exclaimed Sophia.

'I'll take that,' said Constable Crabigail as she tugged the donation box from Barbara's grasp.

'You LURKING LIMPET!' snapped Chloe. 'It WAS you at the bake-off earlier.'

'I knew I should have worn a disguise,' grumbled Barbara. 'Now can someone GET ME OUT OF THIS SWAMP OF SLIME!'

'First things first,' said Olivia. 'I think you need to say SORRY to Grandmer Coral and Chloe.'

'And explain why you stole all the sand dollars,' added Willow.

Everyone stared at the BEDRAGGLED BARBARA until finally . . .

'FINE,' said the stubborn mermaid. 'If you had just let me take over the Tearooms, none of this would have happened!'

'You stole all the donations so we wouldn't be able to fix the Tearooms?' exclaimed Chloe.

'Yep! And then you'd have no choice but to let me to turn it into a BAB'S BISTRO,' huffed Barbara. 'I would have got away with it too, if it wasn't for this DISGUSTING SLIME PIT I fell in.'

'Well, thank *POSEIDON* for *SLIME PITS!*' cheered Olivia. '*HIP HIP HOORAY!*'

'Now we have the donation box back, we can finally *SAVE THE TEAROOMS!*' sang Pam.

'And you, Ms Barnacle,' said Constable Crabigail as she *SNIPPED* away the swamp grass tangled around Barbara's tail, '*ARE UNDER ARREST!*'

Chapter 8

It had been a busy start to the holidays for Chloe and her mermates, but it had all been worth it because they had SAVED TURTLEVILLE TEAROOMS!

With Barbara Barnacle behind bars, Doug began the repairs straightaway. Turns out the bake-off raised just enough money to fix the Tearooms AND buy Grandmer Coral a BRAND-NEW oven.

On the day of the GRAND REOPENING, the whole town came to celebrate.

'Could I have everyone's attention, please?' said Grandmer Coral. 'Thank you, everyone. Without your help, I wouldn't have been able to get the Tearooms up and running again.'

'Well, we couldn't live without your SEA FOAMUCCINOS and SEAWEED SCROLLS,' chuckled Herb.

'Oh, Herb.' Grandmer Coral blushed.
'And lastly, a special thanks to my sweet little ANGELFISH, Chloe, and her MERMAZING MERMATES. When they saw I was in a pickle they put their TAILS TOGETHER and found a way to help me.'

As the crowd cheered, Chloe and her mermates gave Grandmer Coral the BIGGEST HUG.
'Grandmer, you're such a SOPPY SQUID,' Chloe giggled.

Later that evening Chloe and her mermates were chatting and eating yummy cake in the brand-new Turtleville Tearooms kitchen.

'You know, my grandmer is right,' said Chloe. 'I couldn't have come up with a MERMAZING PLAN to save the Tearooms on my own. You're the best MERMATES a mermaid could have.'

'Now who's the SOPPY SQUID?' chuckled Sophia.

'It was nothing,' said Smedley with a coy smile.

'Yeah,' agreed Olivia. 'We had so much fun planning the FISHTASTIC BAKE-OFF.'

'As long as we're working together, EVERYTHING IS FUN!' added Willow.

'And as long as there's CAKE,' said Bruce as he stuffed his face.

'So, what shall we do for the rest of the holidays?' said Chloe.

'How about that TAIL TENNIS TOURNAMENT?' exclaimed Olivia.

'I'M IN.'

'ME TOO!'

'ME THREE!'

MORE

MERMAZING ADVENTURES

COMING SOON

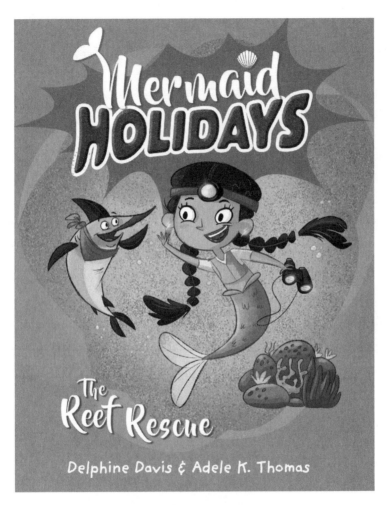

THE REEF RESCUE
OUT DECEMBER 2019

Don't miss out on all the holiday fun!

The Talent Show   **The Magic Pearl**

OUT NOW